© Hergé/Moulinsart 2005

ISBN 2-87424-081-8

Legal deposit : June 2005

Printed in Italy

Note to parents: adult supervision is recommended
when sharp-pointed items such as scissors are in use.

TINTIN
& SNOWY

album **1**

Conceived, designed and written by Guy Harvey and Simon Beecroft
in collaboration with studio Moulinsart

éditions **moulinsart**

Contents

Welcome   8

Tintin and his Friends   10

Tintin's Creator   12

How to Draw Tintin   14

Just For Kicks   16

Crossed Lines   17

Take the Tintin Test   18

Desert Survival   20

Undercover Agents   22

"Red Rackham's Treasure" (Part 1)   24

Crackpot Inventions   32

Marlinspike Muddle   34

Photo Puzzle   35

Jungle Journey   36

Pretty as a Picture   38

Race to the Inca Temple   40

Gangster Guessing Game   42

Wild West Word Search   43

Incredible India   44

"Red Rackham's Treasure" (Part 2)   46

Treasure Hunt   52

Haddock's Insults   54

Out of this World   56

Abdullah's Pranks   58

Secret Island Maze   60

Inca Masks   62

What Am I?   64

Which Character Are You?   66

Answers   68

Welcome

It's time for some adventure and fun with Tintin
and his friends. On the following pages, you'll find
lots of great puzzles and games, learn about some
of the amazing places Tintin has visited and even discover
which character you are most like!
So what are you waiting for? Let's go!

About Yourself

Name: _____

Age: _____

Birthday: _____

School: _____

Draw a picture of yourself

Hobbies: _____

Likes/Dislikes: _____

_____

Favourite Tintin adventures: _____

_____

Favourite Tintin characters: _____

_____

Tintin and his Friends

While Tintin is having adventures all around the world, he meets amazing and unusual people. Here is a quick guide to those who appear most frequently.

Tintin

Occupation: Reporter

Distinguishing features: Tuft of hair (called a quiff) and plus fours

Best friends: Snowy, Chang (first met in *The Blue Lotus*), Captain Haddock (first met in *The Crab with the Golden Claws*)

Characteristics: Courage, intelligence and a sense of fair play

Little-known fact: At first, Tintin had flat hair. His famous quiff first appeared in *Tintin in the Land of the Soviets* when he jumped into a car and accelerated so fast that the wind blew his hair up. It stayed like that forever!

Snowy

Also known as: Morning Snow (by the monks in *Tintin in Tibet*)

Occupation: Tintin's inseparable companion

Breed: Fox terrier

Hobbies: Finding bones

Characteristics: Brave, loyal, generous and adventurous (though secretly prefers the quiet life!)

Captain Haddock

Occupation: Ex-officer in the merchant navy and honorary president of the Society of Sober Sailors (S.S.S.)

First name: Archibald

Distinguishing features: Black beard, cap, pipe, blue roll-neck jumper with anchor design on front

Lives at: Marlinspike Hall

Famous ancestor: Sir Francis Haddock

Characteristics: Generous, quick-tempered, clumsy (and very fond of whisky!)

Hobbies: Inventing inventive insults

Professor Cuthbert Calculus

Occupation: Inventor

Distinguishing features: Round glasses, pointed beard, bowler hat, bald head, pendulum

Characteristics: Absent-minded, hard of hearing and sentimental

Most likely to become infuriated: When accused of "acting the goat" (by Captain Haddock in *Destination Moon*)

Most famous inventions: Shark submarine (in *Red Rackham's Treasure*), moon rocket (in *Destination Moon* and *Explorers on the Moon*), ultrasonic doom machine (in *The Calculus Affair*), colour television (in *The Castafiore Emerald*)

Bianca Castafiore

Occupation: Opera singer

Also known as: The "Milanese Nightingale" (because she often performs at La Scala opera house in Milan, Italy)

Distinguishing features: Floral dresses, large hats, expensive jewels, fabulous singing voice

Characteristics: Grace, charm, immense wealth and a bad memory for names (especially Captain Haddock's)

Accompanied by: Her maid Irma and accompanist Igor Wagner

Most famous song: "The Jewel Song" from Gounod's "Faust"

Thomson and Thompson

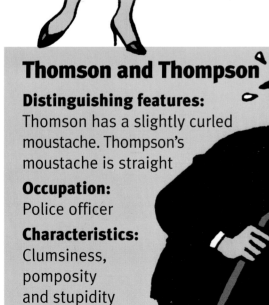

Distinguishing features: Thomson has a slightly curled moustache. Thompson's moustache is straight

Occupation: Police officer

Characteristics: Clumsiness, pomposity and stupidity

Likes: Disguises

Motto: Mum's the word (to be precise: dumb's the word)

Friends with: Tintin

Enemies of: Tintin (they often try to arrest him!)

Tintin's Creator

Tintin was created by a man called Georges Remi. He was born in Belgium in 1907. Remi wrote all his stories under the name Hergé. This is a kind of secret code: he reversed his initials (R and G), which are pronounced in French as "AIR JAY".

As a child, Hergé was a boy scout. He went on summer camps abroad, and learned the skills of scouting. He put these adventurous skills to good use when he created Tintin.

Before Tintin

Before Hergé created Tintin, he drew many different kinds of illustrations for a Catholic newspaper.

Here is the moment when Tintin first gets a quiff!

Life's Work

Before his death in 1983, Hergé wrote and drew 23 complete Tintin adventures. He researched everything very carefully, from ships to telescopes, to make sure his drawings were accurate.

First Adventures

The first Tintin story appeared in a weekly children's magazine called *Le Petit Vingtième* in 1929. The first adventure was called *Tintin in the Land of the Soviets* and was set in Russia.

Tintin Comic

In Belgium, Tintin stories also appeared in a weekly comic. Hergé reworked them before they were published as books.

Tintin's adventures have been published in more than 50 languages, including Icelandic, Arabic and even Latin!

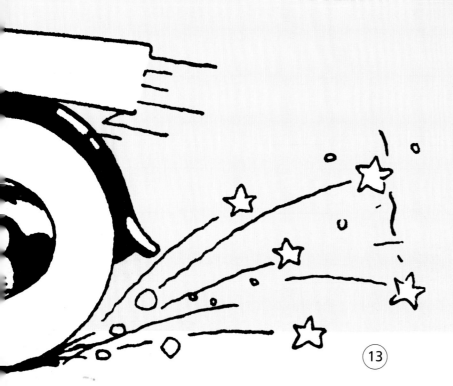

Comic Art

When Hergé began working, many people (mostly adults) looked down on comic strips. Hergé has played a large part in making people realise that comic strips can be "art". His work has been praised by famous artists, including the American pop artist Andy Warhol!

How to Draw Tintin

It's fun to draw cartoon characters, and with these handy tips, it can be a lot easier than you think. If you divide faces and bodies using a grid, you'll soon learn just where to place the eyes, nose and other features.

Scenes

Great cartoon figures need great cartoon scenes. Hergé spent a long time perfecting his backgrounds. Try drawing Tintin in interesting settings, doing different things.

Face

Follow these simple steps to draw Tintin's head and face. Once you've got it right, try different expressions.

First, draw an oval. Trace it lightly in pencil at first, then thicken the line. Divide the oval in half vertically (line x).

Next, draw six horizontal lines to help you place the features. The eyebows are above line 1. The eyes are on line 2. The nose is on line 3, to the right of line x.

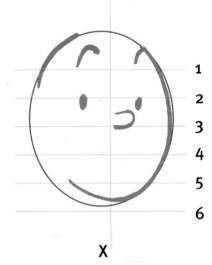

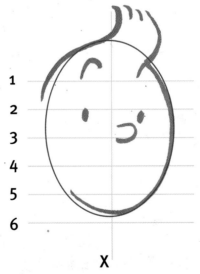

Now you can sketch in Tintin's hair. Make sure it twists upwards from the top of the oval, just right of line x. Note the two small hairs at the top, in the middle.

Now for the finishing touches. The ears should be between lines 2 and 4. The lower lip lies on line 5, and don't forget the smile lines and Tintin's shirt.

Full Figure

To help you draw a full figure of Tintin (or any person), think of him divided into five and a half equal segments, as shown to the right. An important point to remember is that the fingertips reach to just below segment three.

Simple stick figure lines

To help you draw figures moving, try lightly sketching simple stick figures first (shown in red). Then add the body and, finally, clothing.

Hands

You could draw a fab picture of Tintin, but if the hands are wrong it will upset the whole image. One good way of drawing hands is to draw a four-sided shape like a squashed square first. Then add the fingers and thumb.

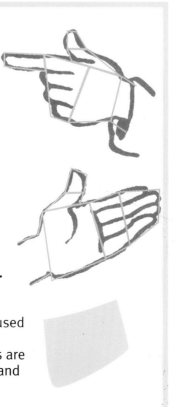

This simple shape can be used as a basis for hands.
This is because your palms are square-ish. (Look at them and see!)

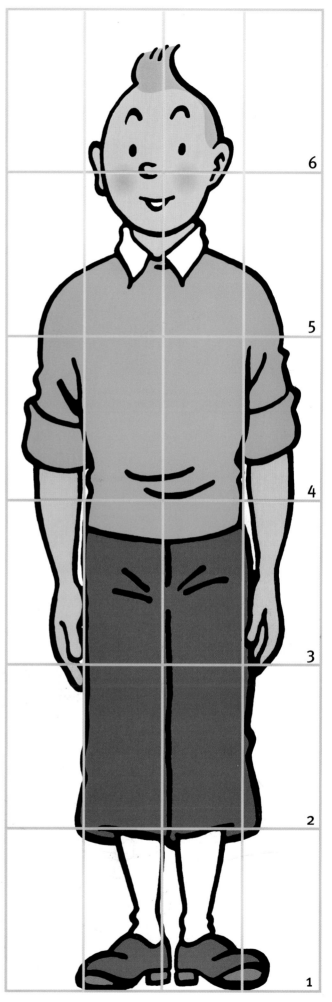

6

5

4

3

2

1

Just For Kicks

Professor Calculus proves his high kick is as high as his IQ when he shows off his sparring skills to moody millionaire Mr Carreidas.
Look at the picture for 30 seconds, then cover it and answer the questions on the next page...

Who said boffins can't box? Calculus gets the attention of the crowd!

Crossed Lines

Poor Haddock. Whenever he answers the phone at Marlinspike, it's either a wrong number or someone he doesn't want to talk to. Who is it this time?

(Answers on page 68)

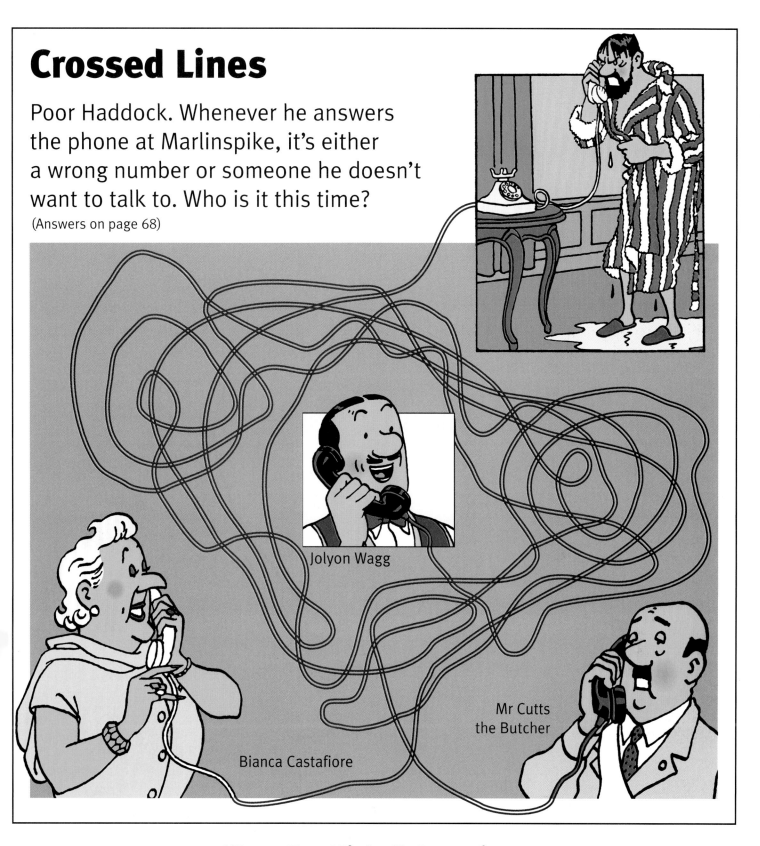

Jolyon Wagg

Bianca Castafiore

Mr Cutts the Butcher

"Just For Kicks" Questions

1 What time does the Professor's watch say?

2 What kind of pen does the Professor use?

3 What colour are the slips of paper in the Professor's wallet?

4 Name three other objects you can remember.

(Answers on page 68)

Take the Tintin Test

How much do you know about Tintin? Find out whether you're clever like Calculus or clueless like Thomson and Thompson!

Part 1: Tintin

1 What is Tintin's job?

A Detective
B Explorer
C Reporter

2 In which adventure does Tintin become a secretary?

A *King Ottokar's Sceptre*
B *Tintin in Tibet*
C *Flight 714*

3 In *Land of Black Gold*, what job does Tintin take on the ship the *Speedol Star*?

A First mate
B Ship's cook
C Radio officer

4 Which of these is NOT Tintin in disguise?

A   B   C   D

Part 2: Friends

1 In which adventure does Tintin first meet Captain Haddock?

A *Red Rackham's Treasure*
B *The Black Island*
C *The Crab with the Golden Claws*

2 Who was Haddock's ancestor?

A Lord Admiral Haddock
B Sir Francis Haddock
C Sir Frank Haydock

3 In which book does Tintin meet Professor Calculus?

A *Red Rackham's Treasure*
B *Destination Moon*
C *The Calculus Affair*

4 Which detective is driving the car?

A Thomson
B Thompson

Part 3: Enemies

1 What is Rastapopoulos doing when Tintin first meets him?

  A Digging for treasure
  B Filming a movie
  C Selling racehorses

2 What is Dr Müller's criminal activity on the Black Island?

  A Smuggling
  B Sabotage
  C Bank note forgery

3 Who employs Nestor before Haddock?

  A The Bird Brothers
  B General Alcazar
  C Cuthbert Calculus

4 What is Rajaijah juice?

  A The poison of madness
  B A truth drug
  C A sleeping draught

A

Part 4: Places

1 What is Tintin's address?

  A 26 Lambert Road
  B 26 Labrador Road
  C 26 Lazybones Road

B

2 What is Marlinspike Hall's three-digit phone number?

  A 421
  B 412
  C 142

C

3 What is the name of the hotel the Captain and Tintin are staying in at the start of *Tintin in Tibet*?

  A Hotel des Sommets
  B Hotel du Lac
  C Hotel Cristobal

D

4 In which of the pictures on the left is Tintin NOT at home?

(Answers on page 68)

Thirsty Work

Tintin is relieved to find water – but Snowy has beaten him to it. Oases are pools of water in a desert. It can be very difficult to find one, though.

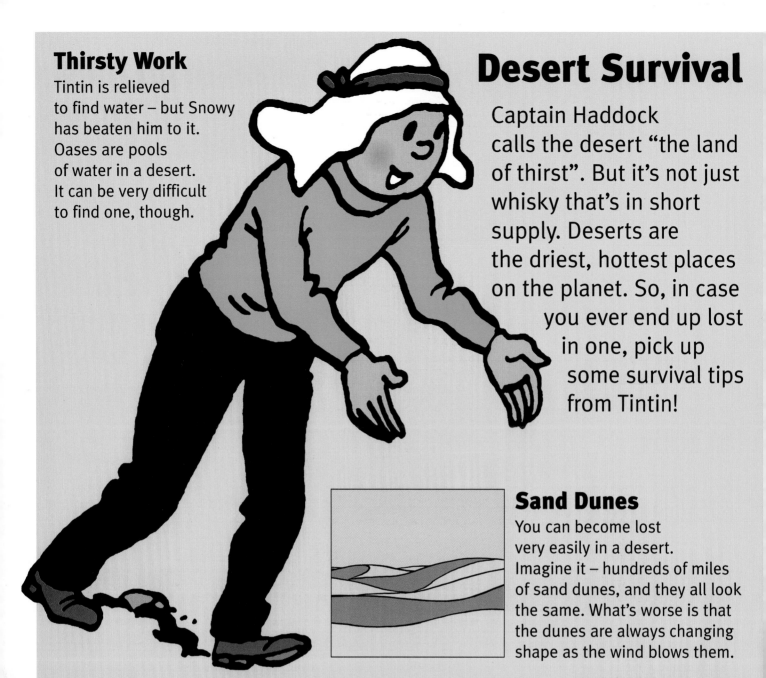

Desert Survival

Captain Haddock calls the desert "the land of thirst". But it's not just whisky that's in short supply. Deserts are the driest, hottest places on the planet. So, in case you ever end up lost in one, pick up some survival tips from Tintin!

Sand Dunes

You can become lost very easily in a desert. Imagine it – hundreds of miles of sand dunes, and they all look the same. What's worse is that the dunes are always changing shape as the wind blows them.

Dinner Date

When Tintin is lost in the desert, he is desperate for food. Luckily, he comes across some date palms. Dates grow in bunches. Each bunch can weigh as much as 12kg – that's the same weight as 12 bags of sugar!

Ouch! A falling bunch of dates gives Snowy a headache.

If you see palm trees in the desert, there's a good chance water is nearby.

Heatstroke

The first thing Tintin does in the desert is cover up his head and neck. His headgear will help protect him from the sun's burning rays. Too much sun can cause a very dangerous illness called heatstroke. It can make people faint or fall into a coma. If this happens, they need water and shade to cool down.

Another dangerous effect of heatstroke is that your mind starts playing tricks on you – as Captain Haddock finds out when he suddenly sees Tintin turn into a bottle of champagne before his very eyes.

Storm Warning

In *Land of Black Gold*, Tintin finds himself in the path of the mighty Khamsin. This strong wind blows over the desert in Egypt and parts of Saudi Arabia. Desert winds can blow the sand up into huge clouds. These sandstorms can make walking difficult. But Tintin knows that the best thing to do in a sandstorm is to sit against the wind and wait until the storm blows over.

An oasis forms where underground water comes up to the surface. Snowy takes a good drink!

Undercover Agents

Thomson and Thompson are masters of disguise. To be precise: some people even mistake them for master detectives. Here are some top 'tec tips to help you look the part when you are on your next undercover mission...

In *The Blue Lotus*, the detectives go undercover in China. But why is everyone staring?

1 Local Dress

When travelling abroad, a good detective always checks out the local dress. Thomson and Thompson's research leads them to believe that all people in China carry fans and every Greek person wears pompoms on his shoes. Perhaps their research is a bit out of date.

What is the national dress in Syldavia? It's all Greek to the Thompsons!

2 Props

Dressing the part is just part of the story. Carrying all the right gear, too, will ensure that no one sees through your disguise. Come prepared and no one will give you a second glance.

3 Local Knowledge

Always "tap" local people for inside knowledge. (Our detectives use their walking sticks!) You'll learn about local customs and hear many "colourful" new words.
Once again, learn from the pros!

As they say,
if the cap fits...

4 The Right Hat

Here's a tip: wearing different hats is a quick and easy way to create a disguise. But make sure you choose hats that people actually wear!

Sailor's Cap

In days of old, sailors tied ribbons to their caps, with the ends hanging down at the back. They wrote the name of their ship on the ends of the ribbons.

Moroccan Fez

The fez is a cone-shaped hat traditionally worn in Egypt and some other countries in the Middle East. They were originally made in a city called Fez in Morocco, North Africa.

Red Rackham's Treasure

ONE FINE MORNING, Tintin discovered a model of a ship at an antiques market. He decided to buy it for his old friend Captain Haddock. The moment the Captain saw the ship, he exclaimed, "Blistering barnacles!" Haddock showed Tintin a painting that belonged to him: it was a portrait of his ancestor, Sir Francis Haddock. In the background of the painting was Tintin's ship! Its name was the *Unicorn*. The vessel's commander had been Haddock's ancestor, Sir Francis Haddock. So Captain Haddock began to tell Tintin the story of the ship...

In 1698, the *Unicorn* left the Caribbean island of Saint Domingo and set sail for Europe. Suddenly, another ship appeared on the horizon. It bore the Jolly Roger flag! Pirates! "Gunners, to your weapons!" shouted Sir Francis.

The *Unicorn* fired its cannons at the pirates. The pirate ship was hit, but not sunk. The pirates hoisted the red flag, which meant only one thing: the fight would now be to the death, no prisoners taken!

The enemy ship drew up alongside Sir Francis' ship in boarding position. The pirates threw their grappling hooks over the side of the *Unicorn* and jumped on board, shouting ferociously.

Sir Francis shouted to his men, "Ayaah! Up lads and at 'em! Till death!" He clashed swords with the invading pirates. Just then, a part of the ship broke off and he was knocked to the ground, unconscious.

When Sir Francis awoke, he found himself tied to a mast of his own ship. The pirate chief approached him. "I am Red Rackham," he said. "My ship is sinking from your cannon fire. So my men are transporting to your ship the treasure we took three days ago from a Spanish ship."

That evening, the pirates sailed to a small island and set anchor. They held a wild party. Sir Francis seized his opportunity: he broke free of his ropes and made his way to the gunpowder store.

Since his own ship had been stolen from him, he decided to destroy it. He lit a wick attached to a barrel...

Moments before the explosion, Sir Francis jumped off into a rowing boat. He headed to a nearby island, where he lived for two years until a French ship rescued him and carried him home.

Haddock continued, "When he was dying, Sir Francis made a will that I, as his descendant, possess. He left each of his three sons a model of the *Unicorn* and instructed them to move the masts of each one..." Hearing those words, Tintin grabbed the boat he had bought in the antiques market. He discovered, rolled up inside, a small piece of parchment. "That's it!" he cried. But the message was in code.

To read it, all three pieces of parchment would be needed. It took a long time to track down those two precious papers, but eventually he did. He lined up the three pieces of parchment: when put together, they revealed the whereabouts of the wreck of Sir Francis Haddock's ship – where Red Rackham's treasure should also be found. Tintin decided to set off and find it!

So Tintin and Haddock rented a trawler: the *Sirius*. On board
was an air pump, a diving suit, and the latest invention
of their friend, the clever Professor. It was a small submarine,
with an electric engine and enough oxygen for two hours of diving.
Now Tintin could explore the seabed without the fear of sharks...

After a long journey, Tintin and Haddock arrived in sight of the treasure island. Tintin climbed into the Professor's submarine. He plunged into the water, and directed the apparatus through an underwater forest of tall plants until, suddenly, he let out a shout...

Tintin could see in front of him a dark mass: the wreck of the *Unicorn*. He returned to the *Sirius*, where his companions rejoiced and congratulated him on his find. He immediately put on the diving suit and returned to the place where the sunken wreck lay.

What a sight!
The ship was
a ruined fortress
under the ocean.
For centuries, only fish
had wandered through
the watery corridors
like silent ghosts.
Tintin spied a chest,
which he took up
to the *Sirius* and opened.
It contained some
mouldy old scraps
of parchment, some
bottles of rum (which
made Captain Haddock
happy)...
But no treasure!

So where was
the treasure?

Continued on page 46

Crackpot Inventions

Tintin's friend Professor Calculus likes to do scientific experiments and invent amazing things. Here are two fun projects that you can try for yourself.

As if by magic, the Professor's pendulum swings towards the thing he is looking for – at least, that's the idea.

Dowsing

Dowsing is an ancient art in which special rods or a pendulum are used to find such things as underground water, hidden metal, buried treasure or even missing people!

What you need

- two straws (or empty biro pens)
- two pieces of coat-hanger wire, folded into an L shape – ask an adult to make them for you

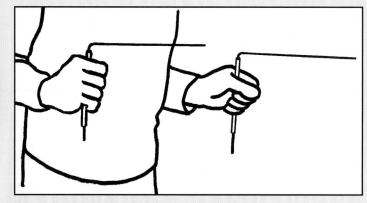

Place one end of each piece of folded wire into each straw so that the wire can move freely. Then point each wire straight out to the front. Now go and explore your garden or your street.

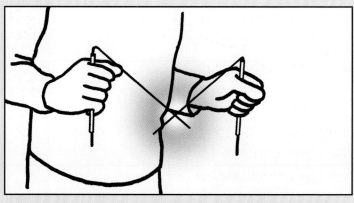

Test that the rods work by holding them over some water you know about, such as the main drain from your house. The pieces of wire will cross each other as if by magic!

Make a Whirlpool

In a whirlpool, water spins round and round as it drains away. This spiral is called a vortex. In this fascinating experiment, you can make your own vortex in a bottle. To see the vortex more clearly, put a few drops of food dye or some small pieces of paper into the water.

The Professor creates his own vortex!

What you need

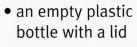

- an empty plastic bottle with a lid
- water
- food dye or small pieces of paper (optional)
- a sink

What to do

1 Ask an adult to make a hole in the bottle lid for you.

2 Fill the bottle about two-thirds full of water and screw on the lid.

3 With your finger over the hole, turn the bottle upside-down over a sink.

4 Spin the bottle at the top, take your finger off the hole and let the water out.

More Experiments

- Try the experiment with different sized holes and with different amounts of water.
- See what happens when you do not spin the bottle first.
- What happens if you tilt the bottle after you've spun it?

How does it work?

The water is pulled down and forced towards the hole in the centre by gravity. The speed of the water around the centre increases as it approaches the middle of the bottle.

Marlinspike Muddle

Do you ever try to tell a story, but get the order of events all mixed up? Well, Tintin's got a similar problem. Can you put the frames back in the right order to show his escape from Marlinspike Hall?

1

Clue:
Start with a breakout and follow the visual clues in each picture.

2

4

8

3

7

5

6

(Answers on page 68)

Photo Puzzle

Villains have doctored two of these photographic negatives. Which one was used to make the photograph?

1

2

3

(Answer on page 68)

Jungle Journey

Jungles are hot, wet forests.
They are also known as rainforests.
Millions of plants and animals live here.
Rainforests are being destroyed
every day, so we must all work together
to save them.

Tree People

Many different people live
in jungles. They have
learned how to live in the
forest without damaging it.
They know which plants
can be eaten and which are
poisonous.

Most rainforests are located near the equator.
The equator is an imaginary line that runs
around the middle of the Earth.

Rainforest people
know how to hunt
and fish without
driving the animals
to extinction.

Jungle Walking

Travelling through jungles is hard work.
You sweat a lot, so it's easy to faint from dehydration.
Locals know how to find water trapped in leaves.
Many wild animals can be dangerous. You have to be
alert every moment, even when resting.

Animal Dangers

Rainforests are teeming with animals. You might meet buzzing insects or colourful birds. South American jungle rivers are home to large, meat-eating reptiles called caimans. This one is being strangled by an anaconda snake.

Piranhas are ferocious fish with sharp teeth. They live in South America.

Plant Life

Plants are important because they produce oxygen, which we need to live. Jungle plants are also used in new drugs that fight illness and disease.

The Captain has been run over by a South American tapir. They use their trunks to sniff out tasty food.

Insects

Watch out for bugs – they bite! Mosquitoes are flying insects. Some species carry diseases, which they pass to other animals when they bite them. Some ants also bite. Others have a poisonous sting. The largest ants are about 25mm (one inch) long.

The Captain provides lunch for a mosquito and an army of ants!

Use the grid on the right to help you draw a picture of the famous Milanese Nightingale. If you photocopy the grid, you can make it larger or smaller. Use coloured pens to finish your picture.

Pretty as a Picture

Race to the

1 Get supplies and start your journey.

2

3 Rest for the night. Miss a turn.

4 Attacked by bandits during the night! Go back to start.

5

6

Tintin's friend the Professor has been kidnapped! He is being held captive in the Temple of the Sun. You must rescue him!

7 Bird-napped! Miss a turn.

Escape from the bandits. Throw again!

8 Daring rescue! Move on two squares.

9 Oops! Miss a turn.

10

11 Approach the snowy peaks!

12 Avalanche! Miss a turn.

13 Warm yourself up! Throw again.

14 Roll back to square 11!

15

Inca Temple

21 Cross the river by canoe. Go forward 2 squares.

You have reached the Inca Temple!

30

Rock won't budge. Miss a turn!

20

22 Look out! Crocodiles!

29

19 Tangle with an anaconda. Go back 4 squares.

23

Behind the waterfall...

28

18 Swamp! Miss a turn.

How to play

All you need is a dice and counters. (You could cut out small circles of paper, and make each one a different colour.)

First to the Inca Temple wins!

27 Fall into the water. Go back 2 spaces.

17 Surprise! Run forward 3 squares in horror!

24

Cross the waterfall.

25

Afraid of heights! Miss a turn.

16 At last, the jungle.

26

Gangster Guessing Game

Al Capone's gang is well known to the police. In fact, just last night, the police received news of a diamond robbery. Witnesses gave them some statements about the crook. Use your powers of deduction to work out from the statements which gang member took the jewels.

"He was wearing a hat."

"The man I saw had a moustache."

"Before the robbery, I saw him smoking a cigarette."

"He wore a bow tie."

Which gangster stole the jewels?

(Answer on page 68)

Wild West Word Search

Tintin is a prisoner of the Blackfeet Native Americans. He will only be saved if you find all the hidden words in the word search. You must hurry!

D	H	U	C	X	C	B	L	S	K	O
W	X	H	S	N	O	W	Y	R	A	F
I	C	E	R	K	W	E	D	S	M	P
L	B	F	G	H	B	B	T	Y	E	K
D	R	L	U	D	O	L	L	A	R	S
W	E	G	A	J	Y	M	D	A	I	T
E	U	A	H	C	L	R	W	O	C	I
S	Y	N	E	T	K	U	Y	D	A	N
T	T	G	W	S	Z	F	O	E	K	T
R	W	S	Q	I	V	O	E	S	L	I
T	O	T	E	M	P	O	L	E	G	N
M	N	E	F	D	S	P	A	R	T	N
A	B	R	C	V	C	A	C	T	U	S

TINTIN	GANGSTER	TOTEM POLE
SNOWY	WILD WEST	DESERT
AMERICA	COWBOY	CACTUS
DOLLARS	BLACKFEET	

43

(Answers on page 68)

Incredible India

On the trail of a secret society that are behind a sinister smuggling operation, Tintin travels to India. This amazing country lies beneath the towering Himalayas. Its scenery is as diverse as its people, with hot jungles, crowded cities and ancient buildings.

In *Cigars of the Pharaoh*, Tintin visits Bombay, the biggest city in India.

Snowy finds himself tied to a statue of Siva, the Indian goddess of destruction!

Religions

India is a land of many religions. It is the birthplace of several major world religions. Hinduism, with its colourful gods, originated there 4,000 years ago. Sikhism was also founded in India. India is home to the world's second largest population of Muslims, nearly 130 million, and Christianity is popular as well.

The Top of the World

The Himalayas form the world's mightiest mountain range. It stretches 2,700km (1,700 miles) across an area in the north of India. The word "Himalaya" means "home of snow" in the ancient Indian language of Sanskrit.

Indian Animals

Many amazing
animals live in India,
including elephants
tigers and snakes.
The tiger is
the world's
largest wild cat.
Although they are fierce and savage,
humans have hunted them almost
to extinction, so now they must be
carefully protected.

Buildings

In New Delhi, Tintin and Haddock
visit one of the most magnificent
palaces in the world – the Red Fort.

Festivals

India is a land of festivals.
Some welcome the seasons,
the harvest, the rains
or the full moon.
Others celebrate religious
occasions or the new year.

Red Rackham's Treasure

(Continued from page 31)

ON BOARD THE *SIRIUS*, the Professor was looking through his telescope. Just then, he noticed a wooden cross on a nearby island. Tintin cried out, "The Eagle's Cross... the instructions mentioned it! That's it! The treasure must be buried there. Let's go!" Captain Haddock wasted no time: "Pickaxes! Spades! Quick – to the dinghy!"

At the cross, Tintin and Haddock started digging, with the help of their two detective friends.

They dug for a long time, with just the chatter of the parrots in the trees for company. But they found nothing! After two days, they decided they must leave for home. The voyage had been a waste of time because they had found no treasure.

On the return journey, on board the ship, one person was still thinking of the treasure: the clever Professor had locked himself in his cabin, and was trying to piece together the scraps of parchment they had found in the chest from the *Unicorn*. Only when he had finished did he show Tintin the results of his work.

Tintin jumped for joy.

It emerged from the documents that King Louis XIV wanted to reward Sir Francis Haddock for his good services, so he gave him a grand house called Marlinspike Hall. Once Captain Haddock learned this, he started to dream of buying back his ancestral home.

This dream became a reality thanks to a large sum of money paid to the Professor for the patent on his submarine. Generously, the good Professor put the money at Captain Haddock's disposal. And our friends took possession of the magnificent Marlinspike Hall.

Tintin and Haddock were looking around the property. They entered the old chapel. There, they caught sight of a statue of Saint John the Evangelist (who is also known as the "Eagle of Patmos"). In his hand was a cross and at his feet, a globe. "Captain!" cried Tintin. "Look at this cross! I am sure that it is the Eagle's Cross mentioned in the pieces of parchment... and here, on the globe, this spot indicates the island we visited..."

The moment Tintin pressed the spot, the globe opened up, revealing a fabulous heap of diamonds, pearls, rubies and emeralds... "Yes! This is it! It's Red Rackham's Treasure!" he shouted.

Thus, our heroes went to the other end of the world to try to find what was so close to them all the time! But they had a marvellous trip and had no regrets!

The end.

Treasure Hunt

Put on your diving helmet
and help search for Red Rackham's
treasure with this fun game.
Take turns to dive to the sea floor,
and then add up your points afterwards.

What you need
- a rod
- a paperclip
- a small magnet
- string
- sticky tape

To save spoiling this book,
you could photocopy this page
or copy the drawings onto paper
before cutting them out.

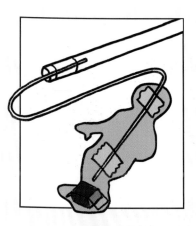 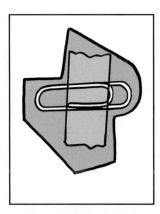 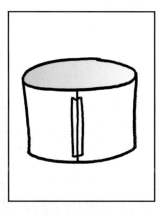 

1 Cut out the diver from page 53. Stick a magnet to the bottom. Attach the string to the rod and diver with sticky tape.

2 Cut out each of the objects from page 53 and attach paperclips to the back of each one.

3 Cut out the picture below and stick the ends together to make a container for your objects.

4 Take turns with a friend to send the diver down to hunt for treasure. Try closing your eyes!

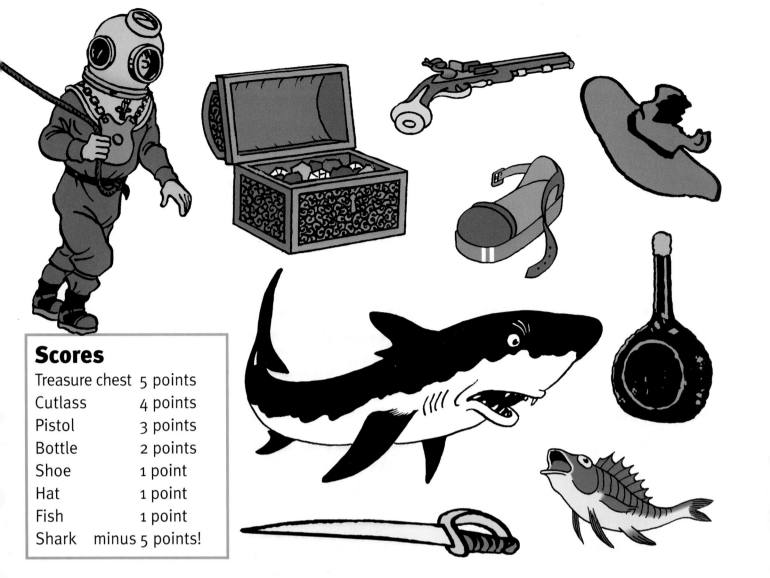

Scores

Treasure chest	5 points
Cutlass	4 points
Pistol	3 points
Bottle	2 points
Shoe	1 point
Hat	1 point
Fish	1 point
Shark	minus 5 points!

Haddock's Insults

Imagine it — you've just caused Captain Haddock to trip over for the third time in a row, and now he's calling you a terrapin! But the worst of it is you don't even know what a terrapin is! It sounds rather unpleasant, but is it? Perhaps it just sounds unpleasant when yelled full blast by an angry ex-sailor! It's time to find out...

For each insult, we've given three meanings. Two are false and only one is the correct dictionary definition. Can you guess which one it is? The answers are on page 68.

SCORE (out of 10):

1-3 Looks like you wouldn't know an insult if it tapped you on the shoulder and said, "Hello, I'm an insult."

4-6 Not bad... but more work needed!

7-9 You certainly know your insults. I'm not going to upset you — just in case!

10 Did you swallow a dictionary when you were a baby?

1 ICONOCLAST

A An ice-cream-making machine
B A movie star's jewellery box
C Someone who breaks religious objects

2 ECTOPLASM

A A microscopic organism
B A ghostly substance
C Someone with a thin body and long arms

MRKRPXZKRMTFRZ!

3 BASHI-BAZOUK
A A Turkish soldier
B A rocket launcher
C A special type of bubble gum

4 RUBBERNECK
A A medical head support
B A way to make a cat purr
C A foolish tourist

5 DIPSOMANIAC
A A person who loves alcohol a bit too much
B Someone who is silly
C A type of dinosaur with giant teeth, jagged spines running down its back and armour plates

6 GOBBLEDEGOOK
A A noise a turkey makes
B To enjoy eating mud
C A nonsense language

7 LOGARITHM
A A prickly fruit
B Music played on tree trunks
C A complicated mathematical formula

8 MOUNTEBANK
A A trickster
B A Canadian cash machine
C One of the mountain peaks in the Alps

9 ZAPOTEC
A A tribe in Mexico
B To attack suddenly
C To make a private eye disappear

10 TERRAPIN
A A water tortoise
B A pretty song
C A fear of sharp objects

Out of this World

Let's blast off into space! But what will we find? Apart from planets and stars, space is empty, isn't it? Well, no, actually – there are space rocks and shooting stars, not to mention Unidentified Flying Objects, otherwise known as UFOs!

Stargazers

Scientists called astronomers use enormous telescopes to look deep into space.

Shooting stars are not really stars. They are small space rocks that burn brightly when they hit the Earth's atmosphere.

Hold Tight

Tintin keeps a tight hold on the side of his spaceship so he is not pulled into deep space.

Free-floating

On Earth, gravity holds us onto the ground, but in space, there's no gravity. This means that people in space float around! Even liquid would float out of the glass, becoming a round ball, like the Captain's whisky here!

Space is the one place from which you can look at the Earth!

Space Rocks

Asteroids are rocks in space. They float around in large clusters. Some asteroids can be more than 1.6km (one mile) wide.

Spacesuits let astronauts go outside the spaceship.

Flying Saucers

This is a UFO. Some people believe UFOs are spaceships from other planets! But no one has proved it... yet!

Spacesuits

Here's what a spacesuit does:

- Gives you oxygen to breathe.
- Maintains a stable pressure (without one your blood and body liquids would "boil").
- Protects you from extremes of heat and cold.
- Protects you from tiny rocks in space.
- Protects you from harmful radiation from the Sun.
- Lets you talk with ground control or other astronauts.

Abdullah's Pranks

Do you want to learn some tricks? Abdullah knows lots and lots! Remember, if you get caught, just remind them your papa is the emir. Unless papa catches you. Then just wail: WAAAH!

Noisy Bookworm

You will need:

- an elastic band
- two pieces of paper (each one 10cm x 20cm)

Roll up two pieces of paper. Put an elastic band round the rolls and twist them until the elastic band is wound up tightly. Place the twister between the pages of your victim's book. Now stand well back! Whoopee!!

Bad Penny

Next time you see someone fishing around in their pocket for their keys, wait until they find them... then drop a coin on the floor near you. The person will think they dropped the coin and will be hunting for ages to find it!

Old News!

Does your papa read a newspaper? If so, save an old copy. Then, one morning, make sure you get to the paper first. Take out the inside pages and swap them with your old copy. You'll laugh at how long it takes him to work out what's wrong. Ha! Ha!

Bump in the Night!

You will need:

• a glass • a metal tray
• dried peas • a small book

Fill the glass as full as possible
with the dried peas.
Balance the metal tray on a book under your victim's bed.
Place the glass of peas on top. Just before your victim
goes to bed, half-fill the glass with water.
During the night, the peas will expand
and drop onto the tray, one by one.
Your victim will think it's a ghost,
tap-tap-tapping!

Silly Straw

You will need:
• a drinking straw • a pin

This is a very simple trick.
Make a small hole in a straw
and then pour some drinks.
Make sure you give the straw
with the hole in it to your victim.
However hard they try, they won't
be able to get any liquid into
their mouth! He, he!

Ripppp!!

Split Trousers

First, find an old piece
of fabric. Then leave a coin
on the floor and hide nearby.
When someone comes along
and bends down to pick up
the coin, rip the fabric.
They will think they have
split their trousers –
while you split your sides!

Secret Island Maze

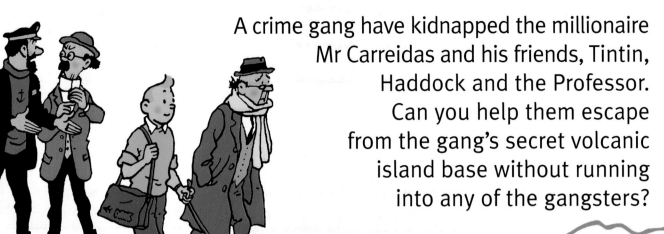

A crime gang have kidnapped the millionaire Mr Carreidas and his friends, Tintin, Haddock and the Professor. Can you help them escape from the gang's secret volcanic island base without running into any of the gangsters?

Rules

- Start at the secret landing strip.

- Avoid Rastapopoulos (the bully in the cowboy hat) and his two cronies – the ex-sailor, Allan, and the evil doctor with the nasty-looking needle.
  If you run into them, you've lost!

- Head for the mysterious bald man with the radio antenna: he'll help you escape!

Start here

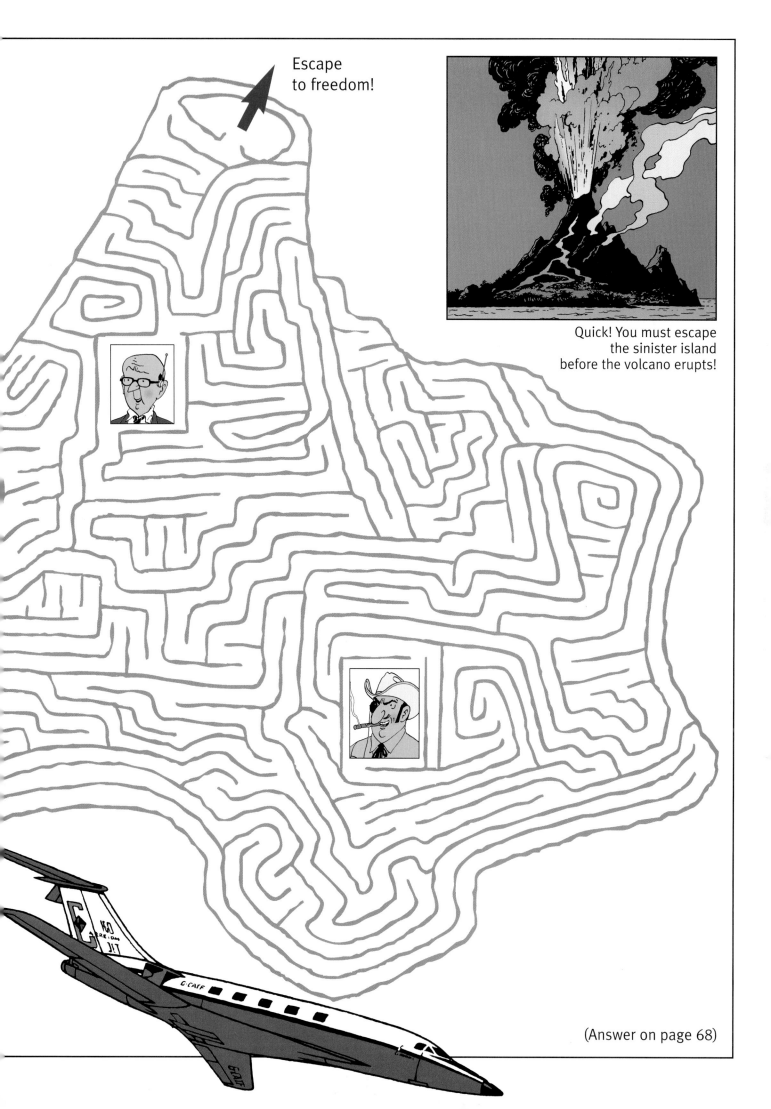

Escape to freedom!

Quick! You must escape the sinister island before the volcano erupts!

(Answer on page 68)

Inca Masks

More than 800 years ago, the Incas ruled over a great empire in South America. The Incas built large temples and cities in the mountains. They were also skilled craftsmen, and made masks from silver, gold and precious stones.

Make a Mask

This Inca mask looks like it's made from precious metals. Use the designs on these pages for inspiration, or invent your own.

What you need

- thin paper (about 23cm x 30cm)
- thick foil (use a foil plate, as kitchen foil will be too thin)
- sticky tape
- a newspaper
- a ball-point pen
- a lollypop stick
- felt-tip pens or waterproof ink

1 Draw your mask design onto the paper. Tape the paper onto the foil.

2 Place the paper and foil on a newspaper. Firmly trace over the design with a ball-point pen.

3 Remove the paper and turn the foil over. Use a lolly stick to carefully push out the shapes on the foil.

4 Use felt-tip pens or ink to colour the foil mask.

5 Ask an adult to cut out the mask for you.

Try adding decorations such as feathers or sequins!

Hergé, who created Tintin, based his Inca designs on real ones that he found in a book. You could try looking in your local library or on the Internet.

Here are some examples of Inca designs.

What Am I?

Here are some of the animals that Tintin and Haddock meet on their adventures. If they could talk they might tell you something about who they are.

Bear

Llama

How to play

Read the statements and try to guess which animal is saying each one. You'll learn some great facts and have fun at the same time! Check your answers on page 68.

1 I can survive for a long time without drinking.

2 I live in the mountains of South America.

3 I mostly eat leaves – I've got a nose for the best ones!

4 I live high up in the Himalayas in Tibet.

Gorilla

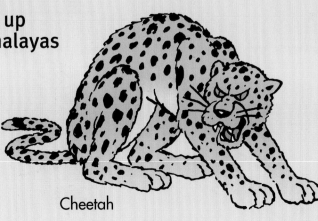

Cheetah

Proboscis monkey

5 If you annoy me, I'll spit at you.

Crocodile

6 I sometimes beat my chest, but only when I am nervous – not angry!

7 I hide under water waiting for prey to pass by.

8 I can run at 110kph (70mph).

Camel

Yak

Which Character Are You?

Which Tintin character are you most like?
Read the questions and make a note of your answer
each time. Then find out at the end whether
you're a great detective... or Thomson and Thompson!

1 **The phone rings. It's a wrong number.
What is your reaction?**
   a) Yell into the receiver
   b) Wonder if there could be a mystery behind it
   c) Drop the receiver onto your foot
   d) Begin discussing a random subject
   e) Sniff the receiver and try to bury it

2 **You're about to drink a glass of water.
The glass smashes for no reason.
Do you:**
   a) Find someone to blame?
   b) Wait until you can find out more information?
   c) Start an immediate investigation?
   d) Catch a train to Geneva?
   e) Get blamed for it?

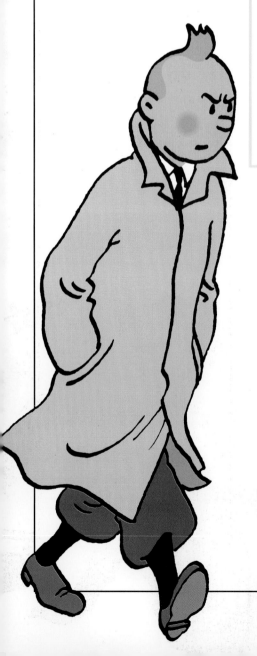

3 **Bianca Castafiore, the Milanese
Nightingale, is about to pay a visit.
What is your reaction?**
   a) Pack your bags and leave
   b) Prepare for the worst but put on a brave face
   c) Make plans to protect her valuable jewellery
   d) Create a new variety of rose in her honour
   e) Swallow her valuable emerald

4 **You are captured by a criminal gang.
Do you:**
   a) Call them foul names?
   b) Work out a way to fight back?
   c) Wait patiently to be rescued?
   d) Call it a childish joke?
   e) Chew through the ropes when you get a chance?

5 **You're lost in the desert. What do you do?**

　a) Think only of champagne
　b) Find water, food and shade
　c) Hope you've packed your swimming costume
　d) Use your magic pendulum to find your way
　e) Look for bones

6 **You're off on a sea voyage to find lost treasure. What do you take with you?**

　a) Crates of whisky
　b) Maps
　c) Sailor's costumes
　d) A submarine
　e) Knowledge of where the ship's kitchen is

7 **A friend is in danger. What do you do?**

　a) Help them – but first point out the dangers
　b) Help them – no matter where or when
　c) Help them – by staying away
　d) What's that you say? Lend me a Great Dane?
　e) Help them – with your terrific sense of smell

8 **It's the middle of the night. The fire alarm starts ringing and fire engines arrive. What is your first thought?**

　a) What idiot started this?
　b) How serious is it?
　c) Run away!
　d) Nothing (you sleep right through it)
　e) Hooray, some excitement!

Mostly a's
You're strong-willed and hot-tempered. In a crisis, you want to find someone to blame. You're Haddock!

Mostly b's
You're resourceful and intelligent. You like to puzzle things out and you also like adventure – just like Tintin.

Mostly c's
You try to help. But often you end up being the one who needs to be rescued. Remind you of Thomson and Thompson?

Mostly d's
You're inventive and individual. You live in a world of your own. Pardon? You are most like Professor Calculus.

Mostly e's
You are loyal and smart, but sometimes ruled by your stomach. You are like Snowy!

Answers

Just For Kicks
(pages 16 – 17)
1. Five to two
2. Fountain pen
3. Pink and grey
4. Hat, wallet, shoe, cuff, buttons, cuff-link, envelope, papers

Crossed Lines
(page 17)
Captain Haddock is talking to Mr Cutts the Butcher

Take the Tintin Test
(pages 18 – 19)
Part 1: Tintin
1. C
2. A
3. C
4. B (This is an old man on board the boat to South America in *The Broken Ear*)

Part 2: Friends
1. C
2. B
3. A
4. B (You can tell because of his moustache – Thomson's moustache is slightly curled)

Part 3: Enemies
1. B
2. C
3. A
4. A

Part 4: Places
1. B
2. A
3. A
4. A (Tintin is in America)

Marlinspike Muddle
(page 34)
2, 7, 6, 1, 8, 3, 5, 4

Photo Puzzle
(page 35)
Negative 3 was used to make the photograph

Gangster Guessing Game
(page 42)
'B' stole the jewels

Wild West Word Search
(page 43)

D	H	U	C	X	C	B	L	S	K	O
W	X	H	S	N	O	W	Y	R	A	F
I	C	E	R	K	W	E	D	S	M	P
L	B	F	G	H	B	B	T	Y	E	K
D	R	L	U	D	O	L	L	A	R	S
W	E	G	A	Y	Y	M	D	A	I	T
E	U	A	H	C	L	R	W	O	C	I
S	Y	N	E	T	K	U	Y	D	A	N
T	T	G	W	S	Z	F	O	E	K	T
R	W	S	Q	I	V	O	E	S	L	I
T	O	T	E	M	P	O	L	E	G	N
M	N	E	F	D	S	P	A	R	T	N
A	B	R	C	V	C	A	C	T	U	S

Haddock's Insults
(pages 54-55)
1. C 2. B
3. A 4. C
5. A 6. C
7. C 8. A
9. A 10. A

Secret Island Maze
(page 60 – 61)

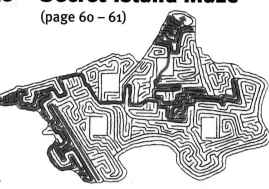

What Am I?
(pages 64 – 65)
1. Camel
2. Bear
3. Proboscis monkey
4. Yak
5. Llama
6. Gorilla
7. Crocodile
8. Cheetah